my doodles, dreams and devotions

Other Books in the Growing Faithgirlz!™ Library

Bibles
The Faithgirlz Bible
NIV Faithgirlz! Backpack Bible

Faithgirlz! Bible Studies
Secret Power of Love: The Book of Ruth
Secret Power of Joy: The Book of Philippians
Secret Power of Goodness: The Book of Colossians
Secret Power of Modesty: The Book of 1 Peter

Fiction

The Samantha Sanderson Series, by Robin Caroll
Samantha Sanderson At the Movies (Book One)
Samantha Sanderson On the Scene (Book Two)
Samantha Sanderson Off the Record (Book Three)

The Good New Shoes Series, by Jill Osborne
Riley Mae and the Rock Shocker Treck
Riley Mae and the Ready Eddy Rapids
Riley Mae and the Sole Fire Safari

From Sadie's Sketchbook: The Sadie Series, by Naomi Kinsman
Shades of Truth (Book One)
Flickering Hope (Book Two)
Waves of Light (Book Three)
Brilliant Hues (Book Four)

Sophie's World Series, by Nancy Rue
Sophie's World
Sophie's Secret
Sophie Under Pressure
Sophie Steps Up
Sophie's First Dance?
Sophie's Stormy Summer
Sophie's Friendship Fiasco
Sophie and the New Girl
Sophie Flakes Out

Sophie Loves Jimmy
Sophie's Drama
Sophie Gets Real

The Girls of Harbor View, by Melody Carlson
Girl Power
Rescue Chelsea
Take Charge
Raising Faith

The Lucy Series, by Nancy Rue
Lucy Doesn't Wear Pink
Lucy Out of Bounds
Lucy's Perfect Summer
Lucy Finds Her Way

Boarding School Mysteries, by Kristi Holl
Fading Tracks
Secrets for Sale
Smoke Screen
Pick Your Poison

Nonfiction
My Faithgirlz Journal
The Faithgirlz Handbook
The Faithgirlz Cookbook
No Boys Allowed: Devotions for Girls
What's a Girl to Do?
Girlz Rock: Devotions for You
Chick Chat: More Devotions for Girls
Real Girls of the Bible
Whatever! Devotions Based on Philippians 4:8
God's Beautiful Daughter

Check out www.faithgirlz.com

faithgirlz journal

my doodles, dreams and devotions

ZONDERKIDZ

Faithgirlz Journal
Copyright © 2011 by Zondervan

Requests for information should be addressed to:
Zondervan, 3900 *Sparks Dr. SE, Grand Rapids, Michigan 49546*

ISBN: 978-0-310-75372-8

All Scripture quotations, unless otherwise indicated, are taken from The Holy Bible, *New International Version*®, *NIV*®. Copyright © 1973, 1978, 1984, 2011 by Biblica, Inc.® Used by permission. All rights reserved worldwide.

Any Internet addresses (websites, blogs, etc.) and telephone numbers in this book are offered as a resource. They are not intended in any way to be or imply an endorsement by Zondervan, nor does Zondervan vouch for the content of these sites and numbers for the life of this book.

Zonderkidz is a trademark of Zondervan.

Cover Design: Cindy Davis
Interior Design: Matthew Van Zomeren

Printed in China

15 16 17 18 19 20 21 22 23 24 /DHC/ 18 17 16 15 14 13 12 11 10 9 8 7 6 5 4 3 2 1

I trust in God becase he is the one
I adore.

All I have seen teaches me to trust the Creator
for all I have not seen.   —RALPH WALDO EMERSON

Dear lord, ~~Mhen~~
can you help me ~~when~~ when
I don't ~~~~ obey and when
I ~~do~~ say no to my mom or dad.
Amen.

God enters by a private door into every individual.
—RALPH WALDO EMERSON

Dear lord,
I praey that ELI will
stop bieing sick.
Amen.

Our greatest glory is not in never failing,
but in rising up every time we fail.

—RALPH WALDO EMERSON

Every man's life is a fairy tale written by God's
fingers.
                              -HANS CHRISTIAN ANDERSEN

Just living is not enough. One must have
sunshine, freedom, and a little flower.
                              —HANS CHRISTIAN ANDERSEN

Love is the only thing that we can carry with us when we go, and it makes the end so easy.

—LOUISA MAY ALCOTT

What we are is God's gift to us. What we
become is our gift to God.   —ELEANOR POWELL

God's greatness flows around our incompleteness;
Round our restlessness, his rest.

—ELIZABETH BARRETT BROWNING

Earth, with her thousand voices, praises God.
                    —SAMUEL TAYLOR COLERIDGE

It's only forgetting yourself that you draw near to God.
—HENRY DAVID THOREAU

The language of friendship is not words but
meanings.   —HENRY DAVID THOREAU

I believe in Christianity as I believe that the sun has risen: not only because I see it, but because by it I see everything else.　　　—C.S. LEWIS

Friendship is unnecessary, like philosophy, like art ... It has no survival value; rather it is one of those things that gives value to survival.
—C.S. LEWIS

_____

_____

_____

_____

_____

_____

_____

_____

_____

_____

_____

_____

_____

_____

_____

_____

_____

_____

_____

_____

_____

We should live our lives as though Christ were
coming this afternoon.   —JIMMY CARTER

Like music and art, love of nature is a common language that can transcend political or social boundaries. —JIMMY CARTER

Once you accept the fact that you're not
perfect, then you develop some confidence.
                                    —ROSALYNN CARTER

Faith is to believe what you do not see; the
reward of this faith is to see what you believe.
                                    —Saint Augustine

Faith leads us beyond ourselves. It leads us
directly to God.   —POPE JOHN PAUL II

The best and most beautiful things in the world cannot be seen or even touched. They must be felt with the heart.   –HELEN KELLER

When one door of happiness closes, another opens, but often we look so long at the closed door that we do not see the one that has been opened for us.   —HELEN KELLER

The best remedy for those who are afraid, lonely or unhappy is to go outside, somewhere where they can be quiet, alone with the heavens, nature and God. Because only then does one feel that all is as it should be.   —ANNE FRANK

Let us have faith that right makes might; and,
let us, to the end, dare to do our duty.

                                              —ABRAHAM LINCOLN

Most folks are as happy as they make up
their minds to be.   —ABRAHAM LINCOLN

I don't know the key to success, but the key
to failure is trying to please everyone.

-BILL COSBY

I know God will not give me anything I can't handle. I just wish that he didn't trust me so much.
— MOTHER TERESA

If a man hasn't discovered something that he will die for, he isn't fit to live.

-MARTIN LUTHER KING, JR.

The ultimate measure of a man is not where he stands in moments of comfort and convenience, but where he stands at times of challenge and controversy.   —MARTIN LUTHER KING, JR.

The future belongs to those who believe in the beauty of their dreams.   —ELEANOR ROOSEVELT

Friendship with one's self is all important,
because without it one cannot be friends with
anyone else in the world.   —ELEANOR ROOSEVELT

No one can make you feel inferior without your
consent.   —ELEANOR ROOSEVELT

You can give without loving, but you cannot love without giving.

—AMY CARMICHAEL

I'm glad we had the times together just to laugh and sing a song, seems like we just got started and then before you know it, the times we had together were gone.   —DR. SEUSS

Today you are You, that is truer than true.
There is no one alive who is Youer than You.
                                        -DR. SEUSS

Be who you are and say what you feel, because
those who mind don't matter and those who
matter don't mind.   —DR. SEUSS

My best friend is the one who brings out the best in me.   —HENRY FORD

A true friend is one soul divided into two people.

-ARISTOTLE

When God made up this world of ours, He
made it long and wide, And meant that it should
shelter all, And none should be denied.

Shoot for the moon and if you miss you will
still be among the stars.   —LES BROWN

To live is so startling it leaves little time for anything else.

                                        —EMILY DICKINSON

[A] mother is one to whom you hurry when you are troubled.   —EMILY DICKINSON

An angel can illuminate the thought and mind of
man by strengthening the power of vision.
—St. Thomas Aquinas

Let us not be justices of the peace, but angels
of peace.   —Saint Theresa of Lisieux

Faithless is he that says farewell when the road
darkens.   —J.R.R. TOLKIEN

Life loves to be taken by the lapel and told:
"I'm with you, Kid. Let's go."   —MAYA ANGELOU

Where there is great love, there are always
miracles.
                                    −WILLA CATHER

Perfect courage is to do without witnesses what one would be capable of doing with the world looking on.

-MORAL MAXIMS AND REFLECTIONS, FRANÇOIS DE LA ROCHEFOUCAULD

I shall be telling this with a sigh
Somewhere ages and ages hence:
Two roads diverged in a wood, and I—
I took the one less traveled by,
And that has made all the difference.
—"THE ROAD NOT TAKEN" ROBERT FROST

Earth's the right place for love: I don't know
where it's likely to go better.
                          -"BIRCHES" ROBERT FROST

The supreme reality of our time is our
indivisibility as children of God and the common
vulnerability of this planet.   —JOHN F. KENNEDY

I want to wear beautiful clothes and look pretty.
I want to smile and I want to make people laugh.
And that's all I want. I like it. I like being happy. I
want to make others happy.   —DORIS DAY

If you don't like something change it; if you can't
change it, change the way you think about it.
                                                    —MARY ENGELBREIT

Always be a first-rate version of yourself, instead of a second-rate version of somebody else.
                                              —JUDY GARLAND

It takes courage to grow up and become who
you really are.   —E.E. CUMMINGS

_____

_____

_____

_____

_____

_____

_____

_____

_____

_____

_____

_____

_____

_____

_____

_____

_____

_____

_____

_____

You never really understand a person until you consider things from his point of view – until you climb into his skin and walk around in it.
— TO KILL A MOCKINGBIRD, HARPER LEE

Courage is contagious. When a brave man
takes a stand, the spines of others are often
stiffened.   —BILLY GRAHAM

_____

_____

_____

_____

_____

_____

_____

_____

_____

_____

_____

_____

_____

_____

_____

_____

_____

_____

_____

_____

_____

Just pray for a tough hide and a tender heart.
                                    —RUTH GRAHAM

You cannot depend on your eyes when your
imagination is out of focus.   -MARK TWAIN

_____

_____

_____

_____

_____

_____

_____

_____

_____

_____

_____

_____

_____

_____

_____

_____

_____

_____

_____

_____

_____

_____

Christians are not perfect, by any means, but
they can be people made fully alive.

-PHILIP YANCEY

There is no improving the future without disturbing the present.   —CATHERINE BOOTH

Our body is not made of iron. Our strength is not that of stone. Live and hope in the Lord, and let your service be according to reason.

—SAINT CLARE OF ASSISI

There is no object that we see; no action
that we do; no good that we enjoy; no evil
that we feel or fear but we may make some
spiritual advantage of all: and he that makes
such improvement is wise as well as pious.

—ANNE BRADSTREET

Promise me you'll always remember: You're braver than you believe, and stronger than you seem, and smarter than you think.
—WINNIE THE POOH, A.A. MILNE

God didn't make a mistake when He made you.
You need to see yourself as God sees you.
                                          —JOEL OSTEEN

You don't choose your family. They are God's gift to you, as you are to them.   —DESMOND TUTU

The Constitution only guarantees the American
people the right to pursue happiness. You have
to catch it yourself.   —BENJAMIN FRANKLIN

Love is like the wild rose-briar;
Friendship like the holly-tree.
The holly is dark when the rose-briar blooms;
But which will bloom most constantly?

—EMILY BRONTË

The fact that I am a woman does not make me a different kind of Christian, but the fact that I am a Christian does make me a different kind of woman.
                                        —ELISABETH ELLIOT

The best way to cheer yourself up is to try to cheer somebody else up. —MARK TWAIN

Sometimes I've believed as many as six
impossible things before breakfast.

-LEWIS CARROLL

I can look at the future with anticipation. And it's comforting to know that someday, as Christians, we'll be able to look back and have a little more clarity on why certain things in life happened.   —AMY GRANT

Your prayer for someone may or may not
change them, but it always changes You.
                                    —CRAIG GROESCHEL

One kind action leads to another ... A single act of kindness throws out roots in all directions, and the roots spring up and make new trees. The greatest work that kindness does to others is that it makes them kind themselves.

—AMELIA EARHART

If your actions inspire others to dream more,
learn more, do more and become more, you are
a leader.   —JOHN QUINCY ADAMS

When you have eliminated the impossible,
whatever remains, however improbable, must be
the truth.   —SIR ARTHUR CONAN DOYLE

Without Christ there is no hope.   —ANONYMOUS

I believe that in the end the truth will conquer.

-John Wycliffe

"Worry" is a word that I don't allow myself
to use.   —DWIGHT D. EISENHOWER

_____

_____

_____

_____

_____

_____

_____

_____

_____

_____

_____

_____

_____

_____

_____

_____

_____

_____

Every great dream begins with a dreamer. Always remember, you have within you the strength, the patience, and the passion to reach for the stars to change the world.   —HARRIET TUBMAN

And this wise man asked me to stop. He said, "Stop asking God to bless what you're doing. Get involved in what God is doing—because it's already blessed."

−BONO

You were made by God and for God, and until
you understand that, life will never make sense.
                                        —RICK WARREN

86

Courage is the first of human qualities because
it is the quality which guarantees all the others.
-WINSTON CHURCHILL

I want to be a role model for Christ in everything that I do. Living my life for Him and showing people the beauty of that reality is my mission in life.

−KURT WARNER

I want to know how God created this
world. I am not interested in this or that
phenomenon, in the spectrum of this or that
element. I want to know His thoughts; the rest
are details.   —ALBERT EINSTEIN

When I stand before God at the end of my life, I would hope that I would not have a single bit of talent left, and could say, "I used everything you gave me."

—ERMA BOMBECK

The greatest thing [people] can do for [their]
Heavenly Father is to be kind to some of His
other children.   —HENRY DRUMMOND

_____

_____

_____

_____

_____

_____

_____

_____

_____

_____

_____

_____

_____

_____

_____

_____

_____

_____

_____

_____

We're so busy watching out for what's just
ahead of us that we don't take time to enjoy
where we are.   —CALVIN AND HOBBES

Nothing can separate you from God's love,
absolutely nothing. God is enough for time, God
is enough for eternity. God is enough!
                                    —HANNAH WHITALL SMITH

Prayer is the opening of the heart to God as
to a friend.   —ELLEN G. WHITE

God gave you a gift of 86,400 seconds today.
Have you used one to say "thank you?"
-WILLIAM A. WARD

Preach the gospel always. When necessary use
words.   -St. FRANCIS OF ASSISI

We can stand affliction better than we can prosperity, for in prosperity we forget God.
—DWIGHT MOODY

Prayer is not overcoming God's reluctance but
laying hold of his willingness.   —MARTIN LUTHER

I think growing older is a wonderful privilege. I want to learn to glorify God in every stage of my life.
—ELISABETH ELLIOT

We can't take any credit for our talents. It's how we use them that counts.   —MADELEINE L'ENGLE

I think one's feelings waste themselves in words; they ought all to be distilled into actions which bring results.   —FLORENCE NIGHTINGALE

101

Each person must live their life as a model for others.
                                                    —ROSA PARKS

God gave us memory so that we might have
roses in December.   —J.M. BARRIE

_____

_____

_____

_____

_____

_____

_____

_____

_____

_____

_____

_____

_____

_____

_____

_____

_____

_____

_____

When we sin and mess up our lives, we find that
God doesn't go off and leave us- he enters into
our trouble and saves us.   —EUGENE PETERSON

Be glad of life because it gives you a chance to love and to work and to play and to look up at the stars.

—HENRY VAN DYKE

A whole stack of memories never equal one little
hope.
                                        —CHARLES M. SCHULZ

Friendships are discovered rather than made.
-HARRIET BEECHER STOWE

Do your little bit of good where you are; it's those little bits of good put together that overwhelm the world.   —DESMOND TUTU

All our dreams can come true, if we have the
courage to pursue them.   —WALT DISNEY

It is the sweet, simple things of life which are the real ones after all.   —LAURA INGALLS WILDER

Throw caution to the wind and just do it.

—CARRIE UNDERWOOD

God loves you just the way you are, but He refuses to leave you that way. He wants you to be just like Jesus.　　　　　—MAX LUCADO

Compassion costs. It is easy enough
to argue, criticize and condemn, but redemption
is costly, and comfort draws from the deep.
Brains can argue, but it takes heart to comfort.
                                    —SAMUEL CHADWICK

We have to pray with our eyes on God, not on the difficulties.
                                        —OSWALD CHAMBERS

God speaks in the silence of the heart.
Listening is the beginning of prayer.
                                    —MOTHER TERESA

_____

_____

_____

_____

_____

_____

_____

_____

_____

_____

_____

_____

_____

_____

_____

_____

_____

_____

_____

I don't want to wait anymore. I choose to
believe that there is nothing more sacred or
profound than this day.
                    —SHAUNA NIEQUIST, COLD TANGERINES

Life is open-ended; there's always more to the story.
                                              —NIKKI GRIMES

I spend every day thanking God for my life by using it the way it seems he wants me to.

—NANCY RUE

I know there's a reason to like every person
here.   —SOPHIE LACROIX, SOPHIE UNDER PRESSURE

I know there's a reason to like every person
here.   —SOPHIE LACROIX, *SOPHIE UNDER PRESSURE*

119

You don't even know how lucky you are to have friends like you do.   —DARBIE, SOPHIE STEPS UP

Faith is alive - it's something that grows
stronger over time. We grow at different rates
too. Don't we all need to see and hear God for
ourselves?   -DR. PETER, SOPHIE GETS REAL

_____
_____
_____
_____
_____
_____
_____
_____
_____
_____
_____
_____
_____
_____
_____
_____
_____
_____
_____
_____
_____
_____

Love is always where it starts with God.
                    —DR. PETER, SOPHIE'S FIRST DANCE

We have to do whatever God asks us to do—
in love—no matter how much it hurts.
                    —SOPHIE, SOPHIE'S STORMY SUMMER

Show God the knots, and he will untangle them.
—INEZ, LUCY DOESN'T WEAR PINK

Dad always said that once you've lost somebody
you loved, it was hard to trust that it wouldn't
happen again. That was why they had God.
                    —LUCY, LUCY'S PERFECT SUMMER

_____

Your mom would be proud of you no matter
what you did, because you have held onto you
and you've held onto God.

-LUCY'S DAD, LUCY FINDS HER WAY

[Jeri] was filled with an incredible sense that
God was in charge of everything that was
happening—that he had things under his control.
                                          —VANISHED

My mom says God will give us boyfriends when
the time is right.   —JERI, POISONED

She couldn't wait to see what was going to happen tomorrow. She knew that with God in her life, it would have to be good.

-SKI TRIP

I have a strong feeling that God has great plans for you.
                                                   —MORGAN, GIRL POWER

I know God had a hand in all these events, just as I know he has had a hand in shaping everything good in my life.

—BEN CARSON, GIFTED HANDS: THE BEN CARSON STORY

_____

More than anything else, I need Jesus in my life. I am successful in my financial life and in my professional life, but all this has come from God and is a gift of grace from him for my life. I will never stop following him.

—KAKÁ, TOWARD THE GOAL: THE KAKÁ STORY

To wish you were someone else is to waste
the person you are.   —UNKNOWN

To love oneself is the beginning of a life-long romance.
                                                    —Oscar Wilde

Ordinary riches can be stolen, real riches cannot.
In your soul are infinitely precious things that
cannot be taken from you.   —OSCAR WILDE

Ninety-nine percent of the failures come from people who have the habit of making excuses.

　　　　　　　　　　　　　　　　—GEORGE WASHINGTON

We ought not to look back, unless it is to derive useful lessons from past errors and for the purpose of profiting by dear bought experience. —GEORGE WASHINGTON

The older I get, the greater power I seem to have to help the world; I am like a snowball—the further I am rolled the more I gain.

—SUSAN B. ANTHONY

Failure is impossible.   —SUSAN B. ANTHONY

Friendship marks a life even more deeply than love. Love risks degenerating into obsession, friendship is never anything but sharing.
                                                                    —ELIE WIESEL

Perseverance is failing 19 times and succeeding the 20th.

          —JULIE ANDREWS

Sometimes opportunities float right past your nose. Work hard, apply yourself, and be ready. When an opportunity comes you can grab it.
—JULIE ANDREWS

So do not throw away your confidence;
it will be richly rewarded. You need to
persevere so that when you have done the
will of God, you will receive what he promised.

—HEBREWS 10:35-36

You don't write because you want to say
something, you write because you have
something to say.   -F. SCOTT FITZGERALD

I try to avoid looking forward or backward, and try to keep looking upward.   —CHARLOTTE BRONTË

I've dreamt in my life dreams that have stayed with me ever after, and changed my ideas; they've gone through and through me, like wine through water, and altered the colour of my mind.
                                                    —EMILY BRONTË

Friendship is composed of a single soul inhabiting two bodies.
—ARISTOTLE

The way you get meaning into your life is to devote yourself to loving others, devote yourself to your community around you, and devote yourself to creating something that gives you purpose and meaning.   —MITCH ALBOM

Forgiveness is not always easy. At
times, it feels more painful than the wound we
suffered, to forgive the one that inflicted it. And
yet, there is no peace without forgiveness.
                                    —MARIANNE WILLIAMSON

Our deepest fear is not that we are
inadequate. Our deepest fear is that we are
powerful beyond measure. It is our light, not
our darkness, that most frightens us.
—MARIANNE WILLIAMSON

And as we let our own light shine, we
unconsciously give other people permission to do
the same.   —NELSON MANDELA

After climbing a great hill, one only finds that
there are many more hills to climb.
                                    —NELSON MANDELA

I've learned from experience that the greater part of our happiness or misery depends on our dispositions and not on our circumstances.

—MARTHA WASHINGTON

I want to live my life, not record it.

-JACKIE KENNEDY

To be kind to all, to like many and love a few, to be needed and wanted by those we love, is certainly the nearest we can come to happiness.
        —MARY STUART, QUEEN OF SCOTS

I am simple, complex, generous, selfish,
unattractive, beautiful, lazy, and driven.

-BARBRA STREISAND

If only we'd stop trying to be happy we'd have
a pretty good time.   -EDITH WHARTON

Through humor, you can soften some of the worst blows that life delivers. And once you find laughter, no matter how painful your situation might be, you can survive it.   —BILL COSBY

I would rather regret the things that I have done than the things that I have not.   —LUCILLE BALL

If you do not tell the truth about yourself you cannot tell it about other people.   —VIRGINIA WOOLF

So we fix our eyes not on what is seen,
but on what is unseen, since what is seen is
temporary, but what is unseen is eternal.

-2 CORINTHIANS 4:18

I will help you speak and will teach you what to say. —EXODUS 4:12

The LORD is my strength and my defense.

—EXODUS 15:2

Now faith is confidence in what we hope for
and assurance about what we do not see.

-HEBREWS 11:1

The LORD does not look at the things people look at. People look at the outward appearance, but the LORD looks at the heart. —1 SAMUEL 16:7

I praise you because I am fearfully and
wonderfully made.   −PSALM 139:14

A happy heart makes the face cheerful, but
heartache crushes the spirit.   —PROVERBS 15:13

Trust in the LORD with all your heart and lean
not on your own understanding.   —PROVERBS 3:5

What, then, shall we say in response to these things? If God is for us, who can be against us?
—ROMANS 8:31

Don't let anyone look down on you because you are young, but set an example for the believers in speech, in conduct, in love, in faith and in purity.   —1 TIMOTHY 4:12

A friend loves at all times.   —PROVERBS 17:17

Let the king be enthralled by your beauty; honor him, for he is your lord.   —PSALM 45:11

Charm is deceptive, and beauty is fleeting; but a woman who fears the LORD is to be praised.
—PROVERBS 31:30

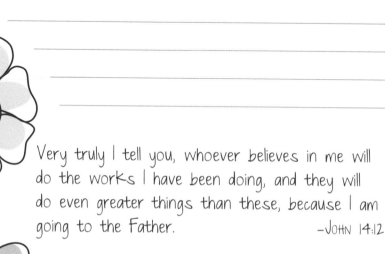

Very truly I tell you, whoever believes in me will do the works I have been doing, and they will do even greater things than these, because I am going to the Father.

—JOHN 14:12

Let us not become weary in doing good, for at the proper time we will reap a harvest if we do not give up. —GALATIANS 6:9

Follow God's example, therefore, as dearly loved
children.
                                        —EPHESIANS 5:1

_____
_____
_____
_____
_____
_____
_____
_____
_____
_____
_____
_____
_____
_____
_____
_____
_____
_____
_____
_____
_____
_____
_____
_____

Do not be anxious about anything, but in
every situation, by prayer and petition, with
thanksgiving, present your requests to God.
                                    —PHILIPPIANS 4:6

And whatever you do, whether in word or deed, do it all in the name of the Lord Jesus, giving thanks to God the Father through him.

—COLOSSIANS 3:17

Love the LORD your God with all your heart and
with all your soul and with all your strength.
—DEUTERONOMY 6:5

His love endures forever.   −2 CHRONICLES 7:6

We do not know what to do, but our eyes are on you.

— 2 CHRONICLES 20:12

_____
_____
_____
_____
_____
_____
_____
_____
_____
_____
_____
_____
_____
_____
_____
_____
_____
_____
_____
_____

I will sing the LORD's praise, for he has been good to me.

—PSALM 13:6

Love your neighbor as yourself.   —MATTHEW 22:39

Don't be afraid; just believe.   —LUKE 8:50

It is more blessed to give than to receive.

—ACTS 20:35

185

I am not ashamed of the gospel, because it
is the power of God that brings salvation to
everyone who believes.   —ROMANS 1:16

Be joyful in hope, patient in affliction, faithful in prayer.

—Romans 12:12

Love is patient, love is kind. It does not envy, it does not boast, it is not proud.

-1 CORINTHIANS 13:4

Love does not delight in evil but rejoices with the truth.　　　　—1 CORINTHIANS 13:6

Love never fails.

-I CORINTHIANS 13:8

And now these three remain: faith, hope and love. But the greatest of these is love.

—1 CORINTHIANS 13:13

Christ lives in me.

−GALATIANS 2:20

So in Christ Jesus you are all children of God through faith.
                                    —GALATIANS 3:26

Be kind and compassionate to one another, forgiving each other, just as in Christ God forgave you.   —EPHESIANS 4:32

So God created mankind in his own image, in the image of God he created them; male and female he created them.   —GENESIS 1:27

The LORD your God loves you.

—DEUTERONOMY 23:5

Be strong and courageous. Do not be afraid or terrified because of them, for the LORD your God goes with you; he will never leave you nor forsake you.   —DEUTERONOMY 31:6

Walk in the way of insight.   –PROVERBS 9:6

Doodles & Daydreams

Space to Create

A drawing is simply a line going for a walk.
-PAUL KLEE

200